Home or Away

John Goodwin

Published in association with
The Basic Skills Agency

Hodder & Stoughton

A MEMBER OF T

NEWCASTLE-UNDER-LYME
COLLEGE LEARNING
RESOURCES

Acknowledgements
Cover: Shane Marsh
Illustrations: Jim Eldridge

Orders; please contact Bookpoint Ltd, 39 Milton Park, Abingdon, Oxon OX14
4TD. Telephone: (44) 01235 400414, Fax: (44) 01235 400454. Lines are open
from 9.00–6.00, Monday to Saturday, with a 24 hour message answering service.
Email address: orders@bookpoint.co.uk

British Library Cataloguing in Publication Data
A catalogue record for this title is available from the British Library

ISBN 0 340 77468 1

First published 2000
Impression number 10 9 8 7 6 5 4 3 2 1
Year   2005 2004 2003 2002 2001 2000

Copyright © 2000 John Goodwin

Typeset by GreenGate Publishing Services, Tonbridge, Kent.
Printed in Great Britain for Hodder and Stoughton Educational, a division of
Hodder Headline Plc, 338 Euston Road, London NW1 3BH, by Atheneum
Press, Gateshead, Tyne & Wear

Home or Away

Contents

Fic – Goo

1

The Letter

Smack!
The ball hit the goal post.
It came from nowhere.
A bit lower and it would have been
in the back of the net.
Then I'd have looked a right lemon.

The next thing I knew
was that the ball bounced off the cross-bar.
It landed straight at the feet
of their number 9.

He charged forward. He was huge.
He was the kid who had flattened me
earlier in the game.
The ref should have sent him off
with a red card.
Instead he was hurtling towards me
with the ball at his feet.
I knew there was only me between him
and the goal.
I went to take a step forward but I froze.
I just froze. I wanted to crawl away.
I wasn't up to this.

'Come on Sanjay,' I said to myself. 'Come on.
You've got to take a step forward.
You've got to narrow his angle
and make his target small.
Keep calm and keep your eye on the ball.'

I was moving. One step and then another.
I tried to shut out the panic from my mind.
I pushed myself forward. He saw me coming.

He stopped and looked up at me.
He had the ball at his feet.
Then he made his move.
He went to his right.
He wanted to dribble the ball past me.
He wanted to lob it into the empty net.
No chance. No way. That's when he lost it.
He kicked too soon.
Instead of lobbing the ball high over my head
the ball skidded off his boot.
It hit me straight in the stomach.
I doubled over and held it tight.
I held it with both hands.
'Don't let it go. Just don't,'
I said to myself.

The number 9 was watching me.
He was waiting to see if I'd drop the ball.
Then he'd be ready to kick it into goal.
'Sanjay … Sanjay,' shouted Harry
out on the wing.

Now was our chance.
If I could pass it to him quick enough
we could break from defence to attack.
My pass had to go right to his feet.
Only then would the break be on.
The ball was in my arm
and Harry was in my sights.
Overarm. It had to be an overarm throw.

I pulled back my arm and the ball
was on its way. It landed close to Harry.
Not perfect but near enough.
Then he was flying in a space of his own.
He cleared one defender and another.
Ryan was in the centre.
If we could score now we'd be on our way
to our first victory of the season.

'Pass it Harry. Pass it Harry,' I screamed.
But I was too far away. My voice was lost.
Still Harry was flying down the pitch.

'Harry pass it to RYAN,' I screamed
as loud as I could.
I couldn't watch
and closed my eyes hoping to hear
'Yeees. ... Gooooalll!' at any second.

I waited for ages but no cry of goal came.
I opened my eyes. Harry had tried to take on
one defender too many.
He had lost control of the ball.
The match finished a 0–0 draw.

'Sanjay ... this is Mr Wainright,
the county team coach.
He'd like a word,' said Mr James
our PE teacher.

'Great save Sanjay,' said Mr Wainright.
'You've got courage.
I'd like you to play for the county team.
We have a tour at half-term.
It begins on 12th February
and I want you to be on it.'

I looked hard at Mr Wainright.
Was this real or was somebody having a joke?
Then he gave me a letter all about the tour
to take home.
I pushed the letter into my pocket
and ran off into the changing room.

2

A Surprise

When I got home I knew something was wrong.
The house was quiet. Nobody was at home.
Most days my sister, Amarjit,
got home before me.
She would be watching TV.
But today the place was empty.

Then I saw it and I knew something
was really wrong.
My mother keeps a jar of money
on top of the fridge.

The jar was empty.
Not one single coin was in it.
I couldn't believe it.
Only that morning the jar had been full.

'Somebody's pinched the money,'
I said to myself.
I ran into my bedroom
to see if anything else had been stolen.
I looked through all my things.
Nothing was missing.
This was strange. Really strange.
I went into my mother's bedroom
to check that out
when the door of the house burst open.
My mother and Amarjit came in.
They were singing and cheering.

'What's wrong?' I shouted out.
'Wrong?' said my mother.
'Nothing's wrong.' said Amarjit.

Then she began to laugh.
My mother began to laugh too.
'What's going on?' I asked.
My mother didn't answer.
She took hold of my hand and started
to dance me round the room.
I pulled her hand off me.

'Tell me what's going on,' I said.
She stopped dancing and pulled something
out of her handbag.
'This is what's going on,' she said.

I looked at her hand and in it
were three bits of paper.
She waved the bits of paper in the air.
'We are going to have a good time,' she said.
'We are going on holiday,' said Amarjit.
'And these are the tickets for the holiday,'
said my mother. 'One for each of us.'

My head was still reeling. 'Holiday?' I asked.
'Where did you get the money for it?'
My mother looked towards the empty jar.
Of course. That's it.
She'd taken all the money from the jar
to pay for the holiday.

We haven't been on holiday for years,'
she said.
'Wow!' said Amarjit and she started to dance
round the room.
'We haven't long to wait,' said my mother.
'It's a half-term holiday treat.'

My heart gave a thud.
'Half-term?' I said quietly.
'Yes – look the date is on the ticket.
We go on 12th February.'
'Oh,' I said.

I wanted to tell her about the football tour –
to explain that it was on
at exactly the same time.
But I couldn't.
Ever since Dad had left us
you couldn't say the word 'football'.
She didn't even know I played
in the school team.

3

Poor Sanjay!

I felt terrible. I was in goal in the next
school football match.
But I couldn't concentrate. I was in a dream.
Instead of seeing the ball all I could see
was that empty jar on top of our fridge.
Inside the jar there was no money,
just my mother's face.

'Sanjay … Sanjay.'
'Look out Sanjay.'

Voices were shouting at me
on the football pitch.
I looked up. But it was too late.
The ball had trickled through my legs
and into the back of the net.
The other team cheered.
Some of their players laughed at me.
It was the softest goal you ever saw.
I had let the whole team down.

'Pathetic,' shouted Harry.
'Rubbish,' screamed Ryan.

The whistle went for half-time.
Mr James our football teacher
took me aside from the rest of the players.
'What are you doing Sanjay?' he asked.
'Sorry sir,' I said.
'You are the best player in the team.
Yet you let in a soft goal.
Are you worried about being a county player?'
he said.
I didn't know what to say.

'It'll be a great chance for you.
There will be talent spotters
at the tour matches.
They'll come from top football teams.
They'll be looking for talent.
Talent that you have.
But you have to stay calm.
Keep your concentration.
Handle the pressure,' he said.

It was then that I decided.
I would have to tell my mother and sister.
They would have to go on holiday without me.
Football had to come first.
This was my one big chance.
It wouldn't come again.

I ran all the way home after the match.
I knew what I had to say.
I said the words over and over to myself.
The light was on in our house.
My mother was in. There was no time to lose.

'I want to …' I said.
'… go on holiday,' said my mother.
She didn't give me a chance
to finish what I was saying.

'Just look at this Sanjay,' said Amarjit.
She pushed a picture into my hands.
'Look at that,' said my mother.
'Blue sea. Golden sand.
That's where we are going on holiday.
A great place –
the best holiday in the world
for the three of us.'

The words I wanted to say
just stuck in my throat.
'I … I …' I mumbled.
'You'll need some new clothes too,'
said my mother.
'You'll have to look smart for your holiday.'

It was hopeless. I couldn't tell her.
I couldn't. She'd won the big match
without even kicking a ball.

4

The Big Match

Two weeks went by.
They were 14 horrible days.
I'd given up on the football tour.
My goal keeping was terrible
and I'd let in another soft goal.

'What's wrong Sanjay?' asked Mr James.
'Nothing,' I lied.

It was our school cup final match.
I made up my mind that I would tell Mr James
I couldn't go on the tour
at the end of the match.
But first was the match. This was a big one.

Mr James spoke to all our team.
'Wear your shirts with pride,' he said
'We can win this cup.
Woodlands is not a great team.
We should beat them.'

Then he looked at me.
'Go for it Sanjay.
I know you won't let us down.'

I ran onto the pitch very fast.
I was determined. I tried to forget
about the holiday and the tour.
I worked hard to push them
to the back of my mind.
All that mattered for the next 90 minutes
was the big match.

We were playing away from home.
A big crowd stood round the pitch
and cheered on Woodlands.
The more the crowd cheered
the better Woodlands played.
The better Woodlands played
the more nervous I was.

They won a corner.
'Come on Sanjay.
Don't let in a soft goal. Don't.'

The corner kick was a good one.
The ball was zooming high in the air.
It was bang on target.
There were so many players near the goal.
I tried to keep my eye on the ball.
Still it zoomed on.
Nearer and nearer the goal.
At any second one of their players
was going to jump for the ball.
Then he'd hit it with his head and
crack the ball in the net.

I knew I shouldn't panic.

I shouldn't jump too soon.

'Now!' said a voice inside me.

I jumped as high as I could.

My hands were high above my head.

The ball was only a few metres away from me.

In seconds the ball would be safe in my grip.

But a Woodlands player had jumped up too.

His head was higher than my hands.

He was going to hit the ball first.

I knew he was.

I could feel him straining
every muscle to hit the ball. I reached out.
My hands clawed thin air.
We both seemed to hang in mid-air.
We were both so close to the ball.
Then down I fell.
The Woodlands player was falling too.
We'd both missed the ball. Crunch!
I landed on the ground in a heap.
The ball was bouncing about.
If a Woodlands player put his boot to it
we'd be 1–0 down. I tried to get to the ball.
But a big foot was there first.

Smack! The boot hit the ball.
I feared for the worst.
'Steady. Steady.' said Harry
as he watched the ball go out of play.
The big boot was his.
He had cleared the danger.
The ref's whistle blew for half-time.
'Thanks Harry,' I said.
'No problem,' said Harry.

5

The Penalty

The second half began. It was a hard match.
With just a few minutes to go it was still 0–0.
One goal could decide the match.
But who would score?

At the far end of the pitch Woodlands had the
ball.
They made a few quick passes.
They broke from defence to attack.
Now they were over the half-way line.

'Look out Ryan,' I shouted.

Ryan went into a tackle.

But their number 11 saw him coming.

He side-stepped the tackle.

Ryan sprawled on the ground.

But on came their number 11.

He was coming straight for goal.

The crowd cheered him on.

'WOODLANDS!!' they chanted.

He still had the ball at his feet.

He was nearly up to the penalty area.

I watched him all the way.

'Tackle him Harry,' I shouted.

Harry took three steps forward.

The number 11 was in the penalty area.

He moved fast. He was almost past Harry.

Harry lashed out with his foot.

The number 11 fell crashing to the ground.

'Penalty. Penalty,' screamed the crowd.

The ref blew his whistle and pointed
to the penalty spot.
Now surely Woodlands would win the game.
I had to save the penalty. I had to.
The crowd was cheering. I looked at them.
My eyes were on two faces in the crowd.
It was impossible. Could it be true?
My mother and Amarjit were in the crowd.
Why had they come?

Before I had time to think
about them any more, Mr James shouted,
'Look out Sanjay.'

The ball had been put on the penalty spot.
Everybody went quiet. I tried to keep cool.
But my head was spinning. My mind was dizzy.
The Woodlands number 11 was looking at
the ball.
All eyes were on the ball.
Everybody stood still.
The number 11 took three slow steps back.

Then he ran forward.
He hit the ball hard and true.
It was right on target.
It seemed a certain goal. Perfection.
I started to move.
Something made me go to the right.
I dived down low.
Somehow the ball just touched
the tips of my fingers.
It skidded off round the post.
The penalty was saved.

The ref blew his whistle
for the end of the game.
Mr James shouted, 'Well done Sanjay.'

By his side stood my mother and Amarjit.
'A great save son,' said my mother.
'But I ... I.'
'You don't have to say anything.
Mr James told us all about it.
He asked me why you had been so worried.
You can go on your tour.
We've moved the holiday to the summer.
There's no football then.'
I just stood and looked at them
with my mouth wide open.
'Was this real?' I asked myself.

Riding on a coach a week later,
on the first day of the tour,
told me it was real enough.
But that's another story.